CoComelon™

ON VALENTINE'S DAY, WE SHOW WE CARE!

Adapted by Tina Gallo

SIMON SPOTLIGHT
An imprint of Simon & Schuster Children's Publishing Division
New York London Toronto Sydney New Delhi
1230 Avenue of the Americas, New York, New York 10020
This Simon Spotlight paperback edition December 2023
CoComelon™ & © 2023 Moonbug Entertainment. All Rights Reserved.
All rights reserved, including the right of reproduction in whole or in part in ar
SIMON SPOTLIGHT and colophon are registered trademarks of Simon & Schuster, Inc.
For information about special discounts for bulk purchases, please contact Simon & Schuster
Special Sales at 1-866-506-1949 or business@simonandschuster.com.
Manufactured in the United States of America 1023 LAK
10 9 8 7 6 5 4 3 2 1
ISBN 978-1-6659-3954-6
ISBN 978-1-6659-3955-3 (ebook)

It's Valentine's Day, and JJ and his friends at school have all made boxes to put their valentines in!

On Valentine's Day, we show we care.
We all have fun; we laugh and share.

They have all made special valentines to give to their friends!

Roses are red, violets are blue.
My valentine says, "Crazy 'bout you!"

Valentine's Day is so much fun!

On Valentine's Day, we show we care.
We all have fun; we laugh and share.

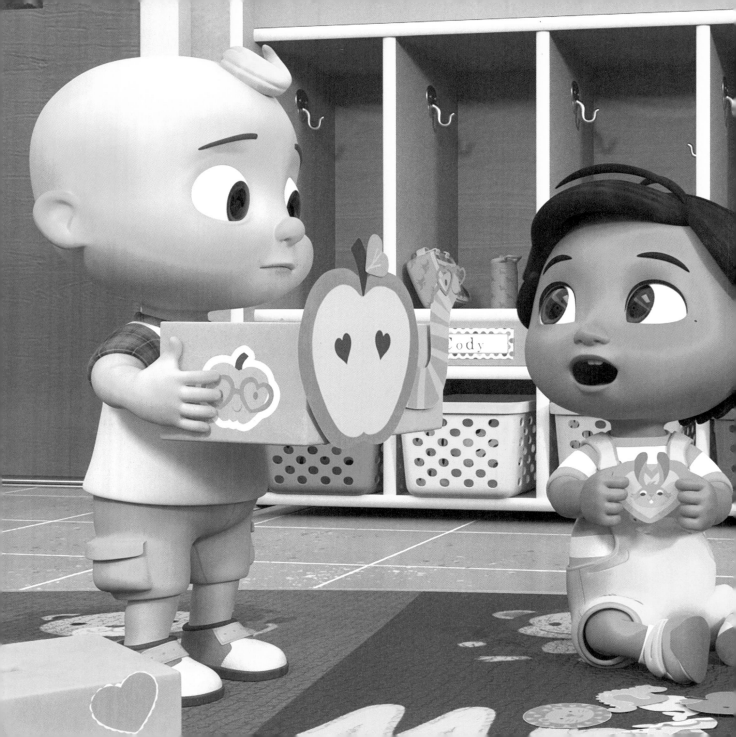

On Valentine's Day, here's what we do.
We tell our friends, "I love you!"

Happy Valentine's Day!